For Julie-Ann, Emma & Mairi

PICTURE SQUIRRELS

First published in 2018 in Great Britain by Barrington Stoke Ltd
18 Walker Street, Edinburgh, EH3 7LP

www.picturesquirrels.co.uk

Text & Illustrations © 2018 Ross Collins

A CIP catalogue record for this book is available
from the British Library upon request

ISBN 978-1-78112-694-3

Printed in China by Leo

Colour My Days

Ross Collins

PICTURE SQUIRRELS

This is Emmy

Hi!

says Emmy

and this is Jeff

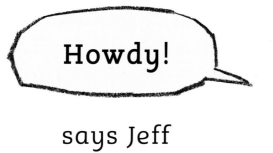

says Jeff

Emmy and Jeff's life was **black**

Spooky! said Emmy and Jeff

and **white**

said
Emmy
and Jeff

Until Monday when ...

Yellow brightened the day

Sunny!

said Emmy

On Tuesday **blue** cooled things down

On Thursday **pink** came to tea

PINK!

said Jeff

Pink

said Emmy

On Friday
green grew
and grew

Nature!

said
Emmy

On
Saturday
purple
sneaked
on in

Investigate!

said
Emmy

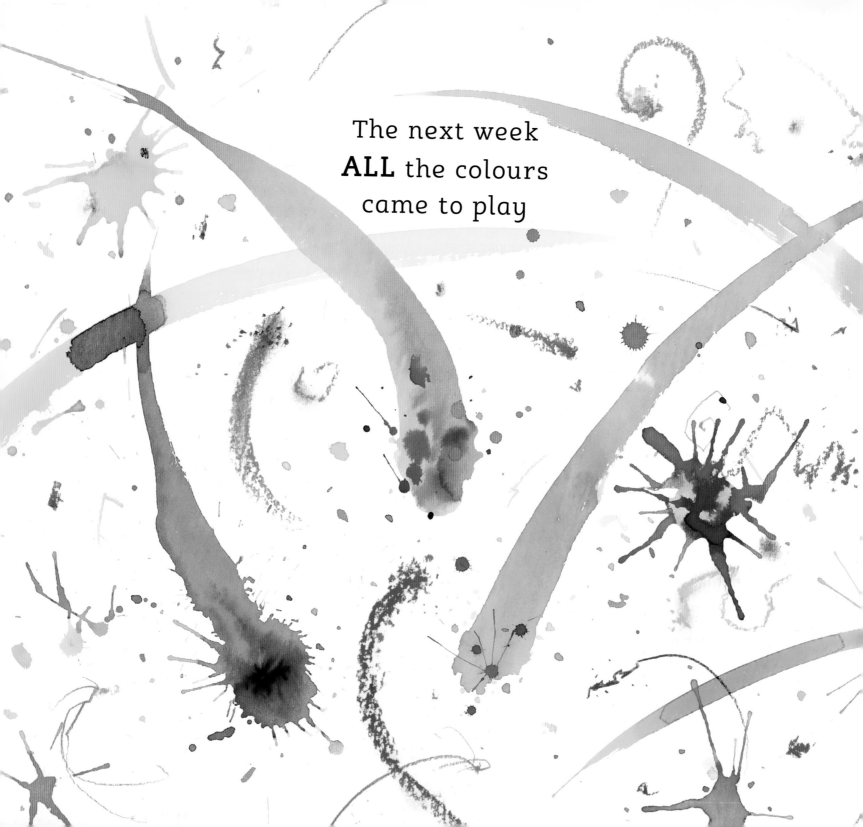

The next week
ALL the colours
came to play

So Emmy and Jeff showed them the door

OUT!

said Emmy
and Jeff

Calm

said Emmy and Jeff

ZzzZZzZ

said Emmy and Jeff.

Grow a love of reading

PICTURE SQUIRRELS